Alabaster's Song

For Austin, Caroline, and Claire Green.
May you always hear the song of Bethlehem.

Managing Editor: Laura Minchew
Project Editor: Beverly Phillips
Design: Koechel Peterson & Associates

Library of Congress Cataloging-in-Publication Data
Lucado, Max.
    Alabaster's Song / Max Lucado ; illustrated by Michael Garland.
      p. cm.
    "WordKids!"
    Summary: On Christmas Eve, a six-year-old boy listens to the angel
from the top of the family tree sing just as he did on the first Christmas night.
    ISBN 0-8499-1307-1
    [1. Angels—Fiction. 2. Christmas—Fiction.] I. Garland,
Michael, 1952–   ill. II. Title.
PZ7.L9684A1   1996
[E]—dc20   96–14749
                                       CIP
                                       AC

Printed in the United States of America

96 97 98 99 00 RRD 9 8 7 6 5 4 3 2

Alabaster's Song

Christmas through the Eyes of an Angel

MAX LUCADO

Illustrated by Michael Garland

WORD
kids!®

WORD PUBLISHING
Dallas • London • Vancouver • Melbourne

I was six years
old when I met
the angel called Alabaster.
That was a long time ago.
I'm grown up now and have
a little boy of my own.
But I still remember
Alabaster.

*H*ere is how I first met him.

y parents always put our Christmas tree near my room. I could see it through the doorway. When everyone thought I was asleep, I would lie in bed and stare at the lights and count the shiny balls. I would watch the color glimmer on the icicles. And I know this sounds a little funny, but I would talk to the angel.

*H*igh atop the tree he sat.
He had feathery white
wings and a golden halo.
I knew he wasn't real. Well,
at least I *thought* he wasn't real.
But he looked so friendly with
those red chubby cheeks and
bright eyes. He looked young.
Maybe that's why I talked to
him. All my brothers and
sisters were older than me.
He was the only one in the
house my age.

So I talked to him.
I named him Alabaster.

I asked him questions about being
an angel. "Do angels have to go to bed
early? Do your wings keep you warm?
Do you ever get tired of sitting on the
tree?" He never spoke, but that didn't
keep me from asking.

*O*ne night when I was in that in-between place between being asleep and awake, I asked just one more question.

"What was it like to see Bethlehem?"

That must have been the right question. Suddenly Alabaster was standing beside my bed!

"It wa*th* wonderful."

*H*is face was round, and his eyes were bright. His golden halo and white feathers glowed and sparkled. He talked to me like we were old friends. And when he spoke he sounded like he was missing his two front teeth.

"It wa*th* a great night. We went to the *th*eperd*th* becau*th* they were awake. They were *th*o ni*th*e. Mo*th* the time they thought we were *th*ars. But that night, they knew *th*omething *th*pecial wa*th* in the air." He giggled with a giggle that made me giggle, too. By now I was sitting on the edge of my bed.

"What did you do?"

"We ju*th* *th*ang. Want to hear it?"

"Yeah," I said.

And from that little angel came the most beautiful music. He put back his head and filled our house with a melody only heaven had heard and only heaven could make. He sang and sang like God himself was listening. I put my head on my pillow and listened until I opened my eyes and the sun was up and it was Christmas morning.

*G*et up!" It was my dad shaking me.
"Come and see your presents."

I jumped out of bed and ran to the tree. There
was everything I'd asked for: skates, a baseball
glove, a train. I was so excited I forgot all about
Alabaster and his song.

Soon all the presents were opened, and we all sat around talking and laughing and looking at the new stuff. That's when I heard the song again. Alabaster's song. The room was full of it.

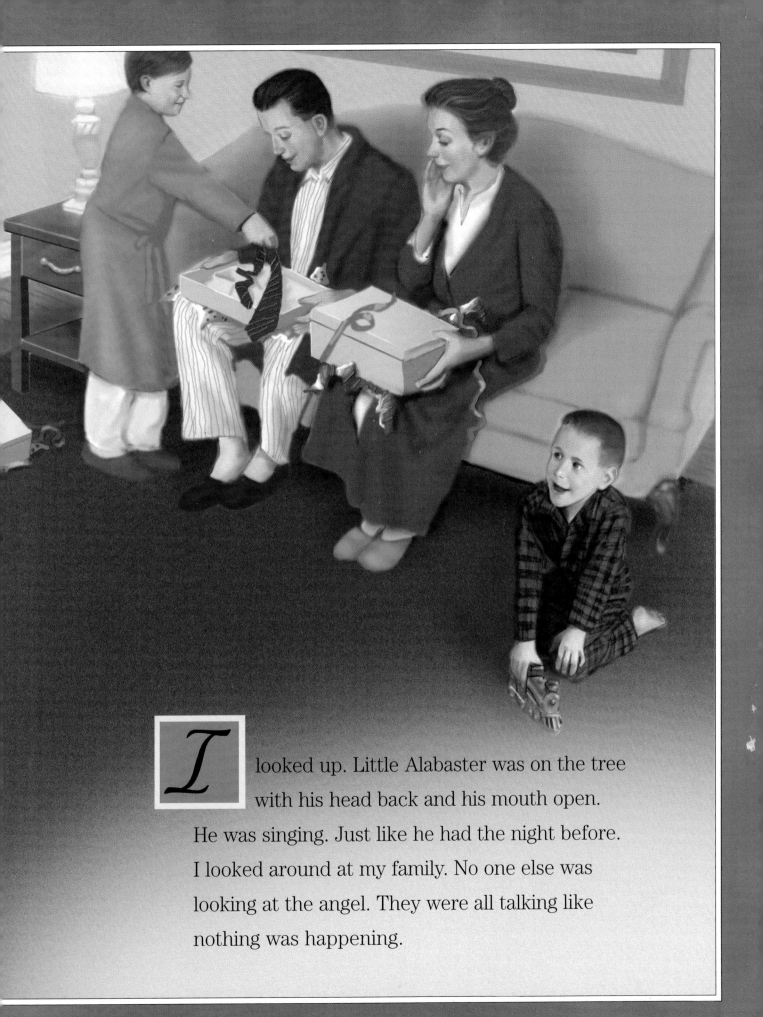

I looked up. Little Alabaster was on the tree with his head back and his mouth open. He was singing. Just like he had the night before. I looked around at my family. No one else was looking at the angel. They were all talking like nothing was happening.

o you hear the singing?"
I asked my dad.

"No."

"Do you, Mom?"

"No," she answered.

No one else heard him. But I heard him,
as clear as if I were on the tree next to him.
His head was turned toward the window,
and he was singing to Jesus, just like he
had done that first night in Bethlehem.

The next Christmas, when I was seven,
I heard him again. And the next.
He would stop at my bed on Christmas
Eve and sing. And from the top of the tree
on Christmas morning, he would sing to Jesus.
Every year I saw him. Every year I heard him.
Then I got older.

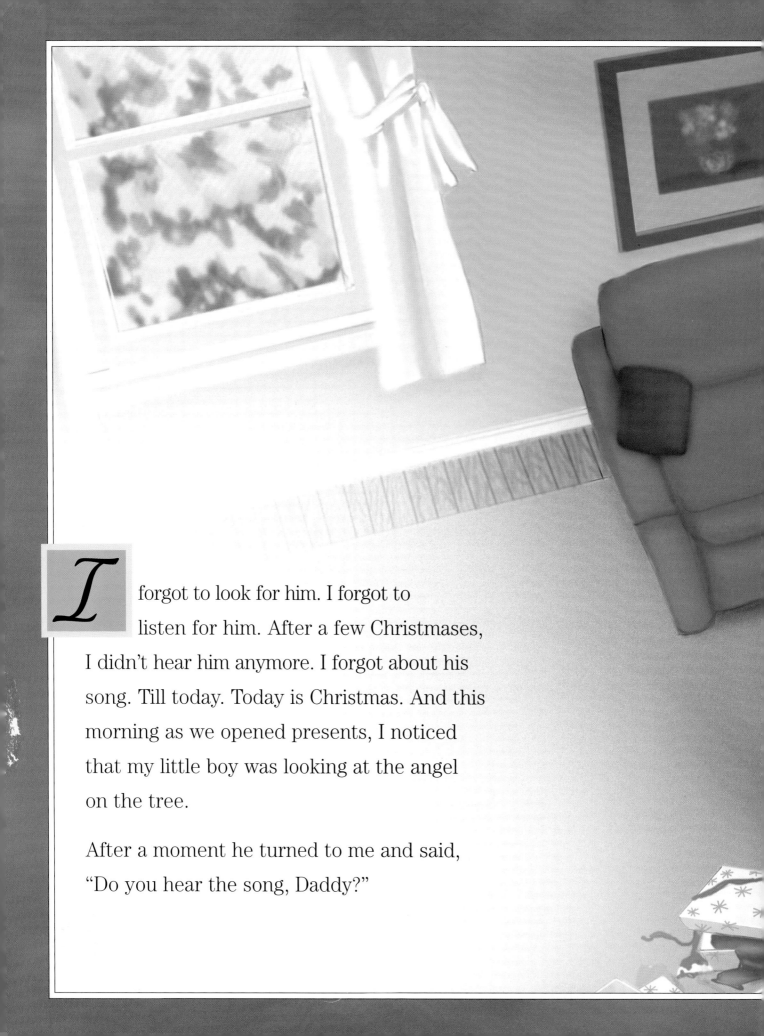

I forgot to look for him. I forgot to listen for him. After a few Christmases, I didn't hear him anymore. I forgot about his song. Till today. Today is Christmas. And this morning as we opened presents, I noticed that my little boy was looking at the angel on the tree.

After a moment he turned to me and said, "Do you hear the song, Daddy?"